To my favorite dancer, Noga.

ISBN-13:978-1505548716
ISBN-10:1505548713

Dancing With The Sun

Written By
Ally Nathaniel

Illustrations By
SugarSnail

"Today I'm a dancer"

Emma said with a smile.

"Dancing is definitely

my favorite style.

I can run, I can hop,

and I can even jump high.

But only dancing makes me feel

like I can actually fly!

My arms are my wings

and I will stretch them so far.

They can reach to places

as far away as a star.

I'm as light as a feather

and as strong as a tree.

When I move around

I feel so truly free.

I'm swirling around

with my eyes closed so tight.

My room is the stage

and I'm feeling so bright.

My heart pumps so fast

as I happily move,

I'm a bird, I'm a princess,

I have nothing to prove.

I can dance high or low,

jazz, tap or ballet.

When I dance, I can feel all my

worries just melting away.

Slow or fast, up or down,

inside or out,

I was just meant for dancing

there is simply no doubt.

My body can't stop,

there's motion in my heart.

I'm a dancer and this is

my number one art.

I will dance every day,

morning or night.

Because that's when my

inner sun is spreading it's light.

Do you know how I feel
when I swirl and dance?
When I do what I love
and proudly prance?
I feel great, I feel sparkly,
I feel fabulously me.
When my inner sun shines
I feel nothing but glee."

Other Books by Ally Nathaniel

Quick Order Form

Fax orders: 612-241-4463. Send this form.

Telephone orders: Call 973-826-2020.
Have your credit card ready

@ Email orders: Ally@AllyNathaniel.com

Please send the following books. I understand that I may return any of them for a full refund-for any reason, no question asked.

_____

_____

_____

Please send more FREE information on:

☐Other Books   ☐ Speaking/Seminars   ☐ Consulting

Name_____

Address_____

City:_____State: _____ Zip: _____

Telephone_____

Email address_____

sales Tax: Please add 7% sales tax.

Shipping by air: U.S.: $4.00 for first book and $2.00 for each aditional product. International: $9.00 first book; $5.00 for each additional product (estimate).

37487602R00018

Made in the USA
Middletown, DE
01 December 2016